THE OFFICIAL LEGO® ANNUAL 2017

Table of Contents

On the Trail

This Kendo Fighter is chasing a thief who has stolen precious stones from the royal treasury. Help the warrior reach the crook by leading him through the maze using the hints on the opposite page.

The Kendo Fighter can only move by stepping on boxes with gems or by leaving no more than one empty box between each gem.

LEGO minifigures™

Finish

Something Crunchy

This werewolf has a very big appetite. Count how many of the different coloured crunchy bones he has gathered for his snack and write the numbers in the correct boxes.

Zombie Attack!

See if you can count how many zombie cheerleaders there are on this page before they start their terrible cheer!

GRRR . . . I'M GETTING HUNGRY!

ZOMBIE TIMES
BRAAAINS!

Web Work

A torn cobweb is unacceptable for a respectable spider lady! Fill in the gaps with the correct pieces from the right side of the page by writing in the matching numbers for each one.

Ghost Hour

Booo! It's midnight and this haunted place has suddenly become very crowded! Look at all the terrifying ghosts and draw lines to connect the matching pairs.

Spot the Difference

Look at the minifigures and
circle the odd one out in
each of the three groups.

1

2

3

The Champion

The greatest wrestler in the whole world of minifigures stands before you. Check if all the parts at the bottom of the page belong to him and mark any that don't.

1

2

3

4

The Queen's Favourite

Lots of brave men hoping to become king have arrived at court to meet the queen. Her Majesty has written down her wish list for a future husband. Read the list and circle the best person from the minifigures on the right!

The Queen's Wish List:

- The king must be fully clothed.
- The king must not have fur or horns.
- The king would never wear blue and green clothes in the same outfit.
- The king must not wear a helmet that covers his whole face.
- I love moustaches!

A Dangerous Task

Help the scientist to put these four dangerous potions away by colouring in the correct white spaces with the colours of the potions. Make sure you follow the scientist's advice on the opposite page. Some potions can't be next to each other – so be careful not to cause an explosion!

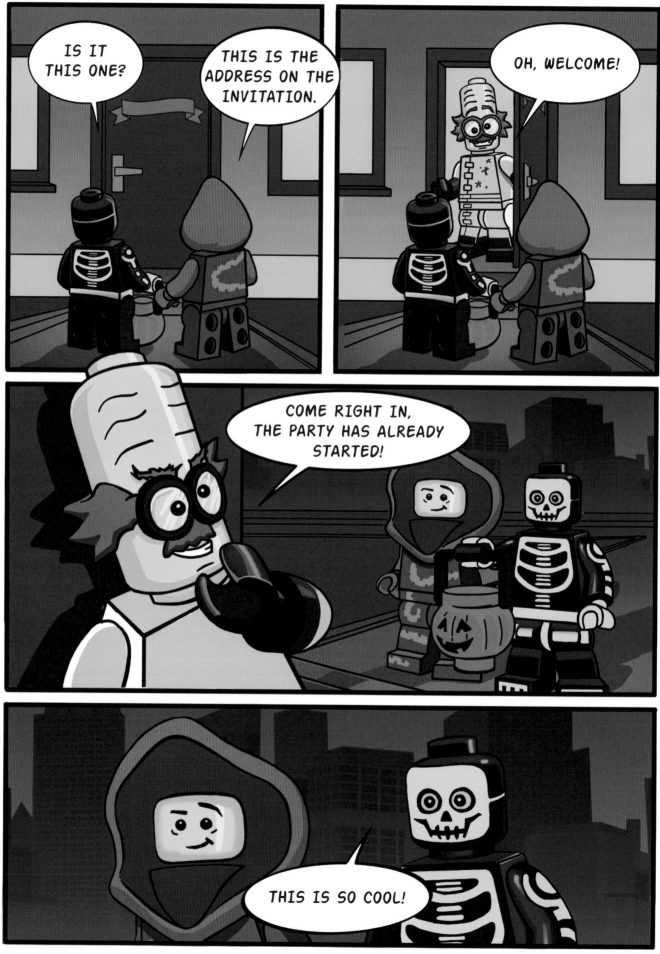

Golden Army

An army of flying warriors stands guard to protect the castle in the clouds. Look closely at each guard and mark the three warriors that look different from the others.

Who's Missing?

Look at the three completed dice below and use them as clues to complete the three unfinished dice on the opposite page. Write the number that matches the correct image on the empty sides.

1

2

3

4

5

6

Monstrous Rock!

This monster can't play his guitar without musical notes to follow! Use a ruler to draw straight lines to connect the matching shapes on the outside of the frame. The lines will cross out the musical notes that you don't need. Reading left to right, put the leftover notes in the boxes for the monster to play!

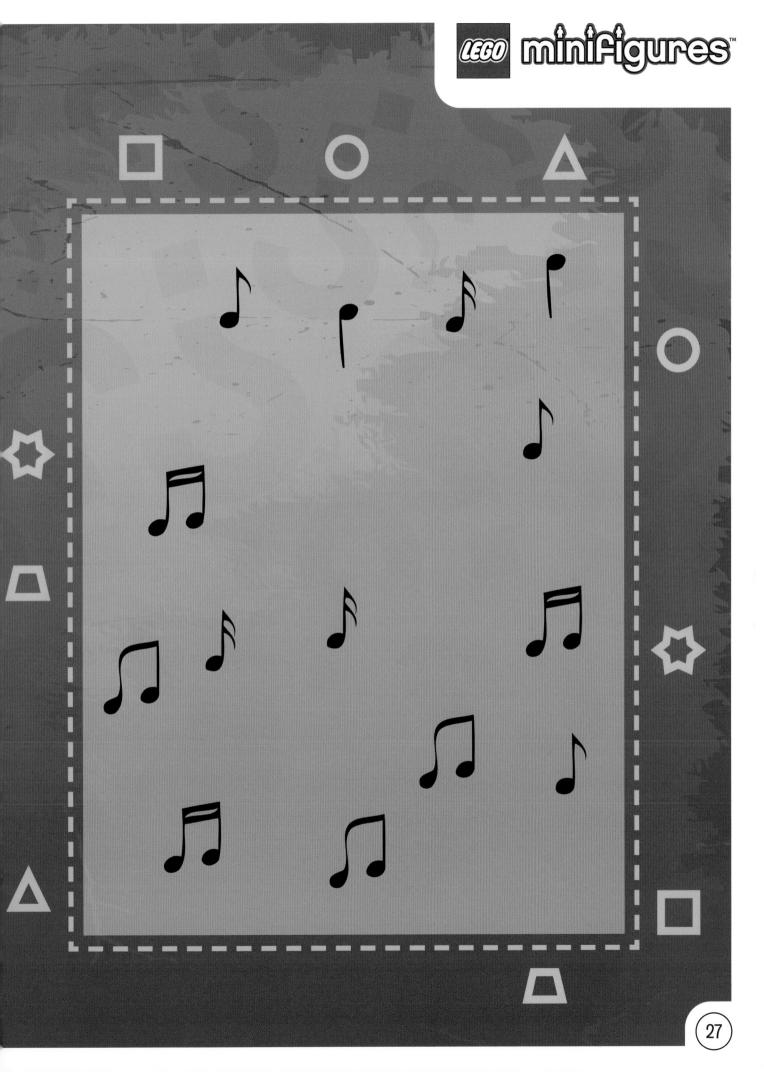

Car Trouble

This vehicle needs some repairs. Luckily, the mechanics are already on it! Match the pictures to the empty spaces and complete the scene.

A

B

C

D

E

F

Important Cargo

Time to become a flight navigator! Locate the landing strip where the cargo needs to be delivered. Find the spot with the same six letters and numbers to the ones in the frame below and follow the line to discover the exact location on the map.

1 a 3
3 4 5

1 w 2
e q 3

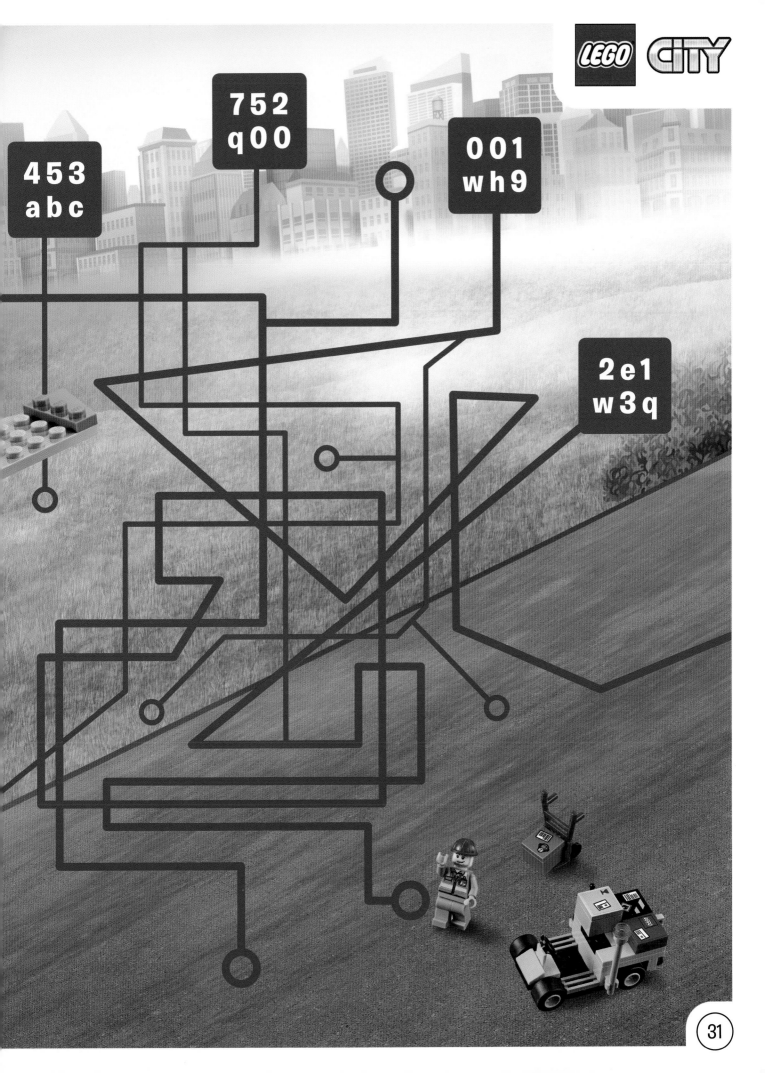

Ride On

The LEGO® CITY citizens all lead very different lives and therefore drive different vehicles. Match the machines to their owners based on the descriptions given by the drivers.

Is Everyone In?

As usual, the hot-dog vendor has prepared delicious food for the firefighters at the station. But are they all at work today to enjoy the treat? Look at the portraits and mark the three firefighters who are having a day off.

It's All Under Control!

Look at these pictures of the firefighters' latest emergency call. Number the pictures to put them in the right order and show the correct sequence of events.

Escape!

Warning! Ten crooks are making a prison break! Help the police to catch them by circling the ten fugitives with a red pen.

POLICE

Crowded Port

Help avoid a collision in these busy waters by drawing arrows to show which direction the ships, the boats and the tyre are going in.

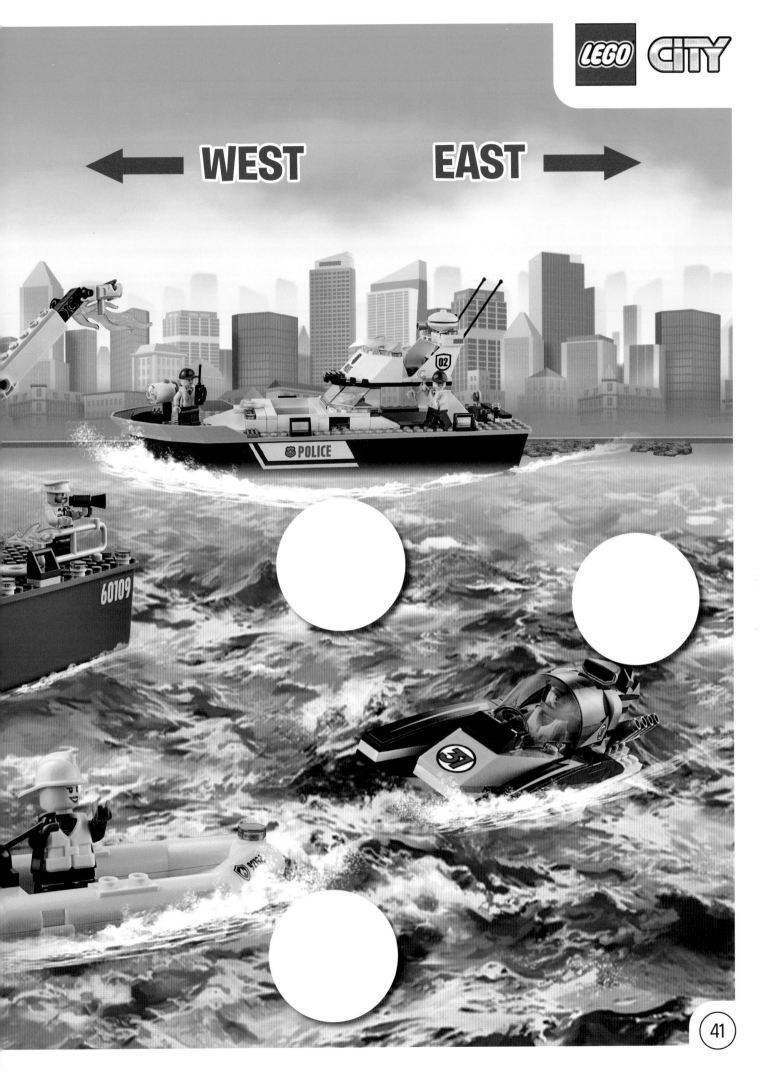

Lava Rock 'n' Roll

Lead the Volcano Crawler machine through the maze so that it collects every pile of molten rock.

START

FINISH

Dirty Work

Finish sorting the rubbish! Place the rubbish in the sorting machine by drawing the correct item in the empty spaces below. Remember, each item must not be repeated in any row or column.

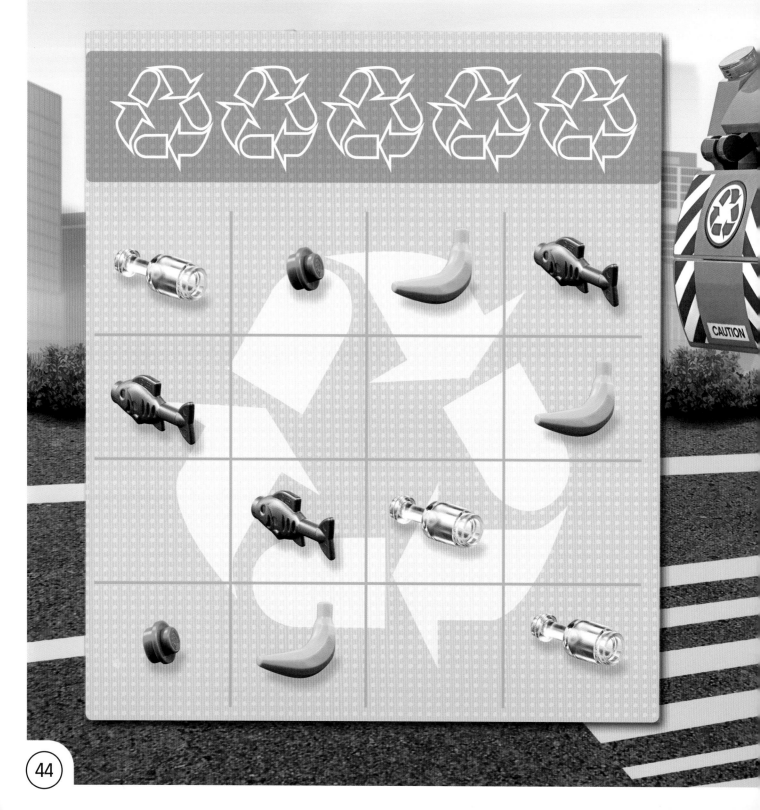

Santa's Visit

It looks like Santa Claus is coming to town with lots of presents for everyone!

Can you find eight differences
between the two pictures?

LEGO CITY

The Perfect Plan

Show Prep

The great air competition is about to start. Make sure everything is in order by reading the sentences below and marking only the statements that are true.

A. There's a mechanic at the airport.

B. No passenger plane is in the air.

C. A yellow plane is standing in front of the hangar.

D. Five jet aeroplanes are taking part in the competition.

E. There's no fire and no oil puddles at the airport.

F. Two service vehicles are waiting in case of an emergency.

Wanted!

Use your drawing skills to help catch this crook! Finish the wanted poster based on the picture held by the policeman.

Broken Indicators

This pilot is ready to head back to base! Only one of the indicators shows the pilot the correct position of the machine in relation to the horizon. Mark the right one.

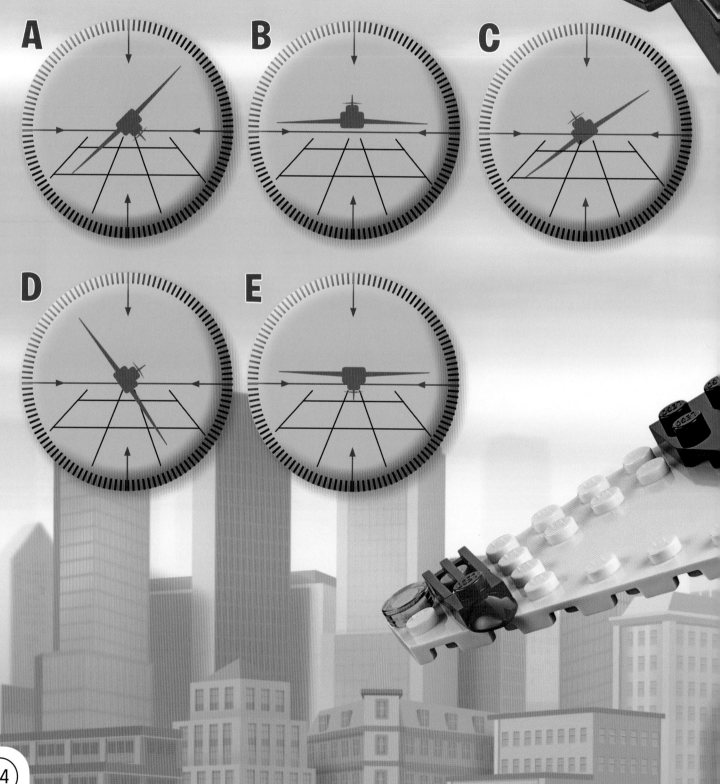

Answers:

p. 4-5

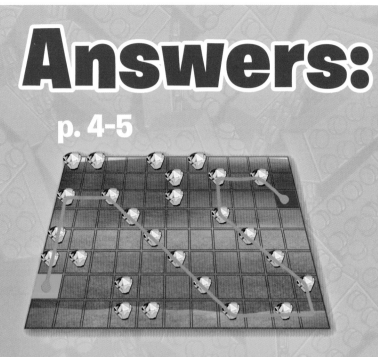

p. 6-7

15

2

4

5

p. 8-9

20

p. 10-11

p. 12-13

p. 14

p. 15

1

2

3

4

p. 16-17

p. 18-19

p. 26-27

p. 28-29

p. 22-23

p. 30-31

p. 24-25

p. 32-33

p. 34-35

p. 36-37

p. 38-39

p. 40-41

p. 42-43

p. 44-45

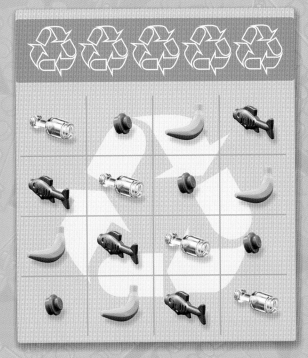

p. 46-47

p. 50-51

A, B, E

p. 54-55

C